BOOKS BY TIM MCBAIN & L.T. VARGUS

Casting Shadows Everywhere

The Awake in the Dark series

The Scattered and the Dead series

The Clowns

The Violet Darger series

The Victor Loshak series

IMAGE IN A CRACKED MIRROR

IMAGE IN A CRACKED MIRROR

a Violet Darger novella

LT VARGUS & TIM MCBAIN

SMARMY PRESS

IMAGE IN A CRACKED MIRROR

Unfortunately, this story is based on a real case. While we took liberties with certain aspects, many of the details remain true to life, including everything from the grisly stuff to the mac and cheese.

CHAPTER 1

It was six minutes after 11 PM when Darger's phone chirped on the coffee table. She checked it, a tad surprised to find Victor Loshak's name on the display screen, especially at this hour. Weird. But then she remembered. He'd offered to get her the Leonard Stump file. He must be following through on that, a prospect that excited her more than she wanted to admit to herself. In the weeks since she'd returned from Ohio, she'd spent many hours imagining what horrors and secrets those pages must contain.

She slid the tip of her tongue over her lips in one last tick of hesitation, and then she thumbed the green button and brought the phone to her ear.

"Special Agent Loshak… Isn't it past your bed time?"

There was a pause on the other end, and then she realized she could hear Loshak's wheezy laugh. It was like an endless stream of inhales. More like labored breathing than real laughter.

"Smart ass," he said, finally. "Look, I've got something I think you'll be interested in. I'm about to fly out on a case — a real ghastly one — and it's a bit of an emergency."

Darger's mind raced, still trying to figure out how this thread of conversation would lead to him offering to send over the file she'd been building up in her head over these past few weeks.

"A family of four got murdered on Lopez Island — a little, rural community off the coast of Washington state," Loshak continued. "We're talking four brutal stabbings, including two children — a 6-year-old and an infant."

"Jesus."

"Yeah. All the mirrors in the house had been shattered, and bizarre mutilations were performed postmortem. Mostly on the adults, although… Maybe I ought to wait to get into the, uh, details of the thing."

They were quiet for a beat before Loshak resumed talking. Darger found herself oddly conscious of her breathing. Worried that she may be exhaling into the phone's microphone like some creepy crank caller.

"The locals are pretty spooked, naturally, and the San Juan County Sheriff's department isn't quite sure how to proceed. It's a pretty unique situation. They were able to tie a few suspects — five, I believe — to the scene on the evening of the crime, but they don't necessarily have enough to get a warrant on any of them. They've asked me to fly in, go over the crime scenes and come up with a profile that they can use to convince a judge to allow a search."

"I see," she said, still wondering how this related to the Leonard Stump file.

"All of the suspects are in custody now, but I've only got about 18 hours to sort it all out before they'll be cut loose. Anyhow, I reserved a ticket for you, if you want to come. I kind of figured you could look over the case files on the flight, and we'd go from there. Two heads are better than one and all of that."

Again, Darger focused on her breathing, feeling the sharp tendril of cold enter her throat and chest as she gasped a little. It took her a second to wrangle her vocal cords into answering the man.

"But… I thought…"

"You're worried about the bureaucratic BS?"

"Yeah. A little," she admitted. It was the other thing that had been occupying her mind lately: when — not if — she'd be penalized by those she'd disobeyed. She had, after all, committed blatant insubordination with the Athens case. She couldn't deny it.

"Well, don't. This is way above Ryskamp and his cronies. I got the OK from someone farther up the chain."

For a second, Darger regretted that she wouldn't get the Stump file. But this opportunity was something much better. Wasn't it?

"Sure. Yeah. What time's the flight?"

CHAPTER 2

With a population of just under 2,200 souls strewn over 29.8 square miles, Lopez Island looked more like a slice of forest set a few miles off the coast than it did a likely site for a violent crime. It was rural. Scenic. Peaceful.

Darger and Loshak arrived by ferry, driving their rental car — a Nissan Altima — off the boat at the landing and immediately finding trees lining both sides of the road. Thick woods and farmland occupied the landscape for most of their drive with residences only periodically breaking up the foliage.

"Seems like a nice enough place," Loshak said.

He ran a hand through his salt and pepper hair which drew back from his forehead in that receding horseshoe-shape male pattern baldness sometimes enforced. Aviator sunglasses covered his eyes, so Darger couldn't read him very well for the moment.

"You know, retirement isn't so far off for me now," he said. "I wouldn't mind living someplace like this, maybe. When the time comes."

The Bureau's bylaws included a mandatory retirement at 57 years old, strictly enforced, Darger knew, so Loshak was already in his final years as an agent. That seemed hard for her to believe. Pancreatitis hadn't stopped him. It didn't seem like age could. Not anytime soon.

He must have noticed her smirking to herself,

because he turned and aimed the reflective lenses of his sunglasses at her.

"Is that funny?" he asked.

She shook her head.

"I'm just having a hard time picturing you relaxing in a hammock all day. Enjoying sunsets. Golfing?"

He adjusted his grip on the steering wheel, shrugging.

"Just a passing thought, really. Lots of coastline and woods to explore is all. I could figure out how to fish or something."

The houses they passed were mostly large and modern builds. Angular lines in metal and natural wood. Plenty of windows to take advantage of the views. The Douglas firs and Oregon oaks towered over the more normal-looking houses, while the mansions seemed to have more manicured lawns, exotic grasses and shrubs running just along the borders of things, trimmed to perfection in a way that reminded her of fussy facial hair.

The Altima rounded a corner, and suddenly the ocean came back into view, waves lapping at the back doors of the beach front homes on this side of the island. The sand and sea seemed to be in odd proximity to the houses nestled back into the woods. And if there were any downtown type area on this little piece of land, she hadn't seen it, nor could she picture how it'd fit in. There must be a convenience store and a gas station, at least, though. Right?

When Loshak steered the car onto a winding blacktop driveway, she knew they must be at the location. Pines taller and thicker than anything she'd ever seen back east stood along the asphalt strip, and the dried out needles formed a brown carpet beneath them.

The house came into view at the end of the bend, looking like nothing special at first — a single story home with beige vinyl siding that sat at the bottom of a hill, nestled among the trees. But then she looked past the home and saw that the land fell away just there. It was practically hanging over the ocean. She'd never seen a house quite like it — woods on one side, ocean on the other.

Loshak parked the car at the end of the driveway, the engine's growl cutting out to silence, and they both craned their necks for a moment to survey the landscape.

"Sure doesn't look like a murder scene," she said.

"No. But then, most of them don't. 'Til you get inside, anyway."

They were quiet for a beat, and tension gripped Darger's chest, clenching the muscles around her sternum. For some reason, she was reluctant to get out of the car, and Loshak seemed to be hesitating as well.

"I take it you got a look at the files on the plane?" he said. "Any initial thoughts?"

He'd slept the whole flight, his eyes blindfolded, his chin resting on one of those foam neck pillows. She'd read the file to the sound of his breath scraping in and out of him, thick and raspy, somehow falling below a snore if just barely.

She had sat in the window seat on the plane, which

offered her some small sense of privacy. It felt strange, still, looking through grisly photos among all of those passengers, flight attendants walking up and down the aisle handing out ginger ale and pretzels. Even though she knew no one could see the photographs, she flipped through them quickly, holding her breath all the while and barely taking them in apart from the red and wet bits. Something about that made the process feel incomplete. Half digested, she thought, for lack of a more appropriate term.

"Yeah," she said. "But I think I'd rather take a look around the house first before we discuss it. If you don't mind, that is."

A mysterious half-smile curved the corners of Loshak's mouth, and once more she found herself wishing he weren't wearing the aviators like some kind of poker pro.

"Just as well," he said after a pause. "I don't mind at all."

She took what she sensed was a rare opportunity to study him as they walked toward the house. Victor Loshak in his natural habitat.

He was thinner than when they'd first met, that was for sure. He'd lost weight during his time in the hospital. But his skin had a healthy pinkness to it that had been entirely absent in their time in Ohio. A rosy glow. That was something, at least.

Police tape fluttered in the breeze just beyond the car's hood, smacking against the tree trunk it had been wrapped around. The yellow tape formed a rectangular perimeter around the house and most of the yard.

Loshak pinched it carefully between his thumb and fingers and pulled it up into a little peak to make it easier for Darger to duck under.

As they walked through the yard, the light was bright around them despite a lack of sunshine — a gray gleam that came from nowhere and somehow shined everywhere. Even the lodgepole pines that towered over everything in the vicinity seemed to cast no shadows.

A sweet, woody smell surrounded them. It made her think of pine sap, though she wasn't sure that's what it was.

Standing at the back corner of the home, her eyes finished the journey for her, skimming down the slope to the place where the water met the land. The way the dense woods severed all at once into that open air over the ocean was even more striking up close, and the air swirled off of the water just then, picking up strands of her hair.

Despite the wind, the sea was calm. It lay flat from here to the neighboring island on the horizon — San Juan Island, she thought. The faintest ripples stirred on the surface. It looked more tranquil than any oceanfront view she'd ever seen, in fact — in real life or on TV.

"Weird how still it is, eh?" Loshak said behind her, his shoulders squared at the same view. "The water between the islands is more like bathwater than any kind of raging sea."

She thought on it a moment and nodded.

The wind picked up again, a bigger gust this time,

tousling Loshak's hair and whipping hers into her eyes. They faced it down, and when it died out, Loshak spoke.

"Should we go inside?"

Finally, she turned away from the water, tearing her gaze from the mirror-like surface of the bay.

"Yeah. Better take a look."

CHAPTER 3

Loshak peeled down the criss-crossing police tape that formed an X over the front door and let it fall to the ground. It lay on the linoleum, partially coiled there like a dead snake. They milled around in the foyer a moment — surrounded by shoes and jackets and a purse. Darger noted the sheer tininess of a pair of white Keds on the floor and felt the need to change the subject.

"Whoever it was, they didn't take the purse," she said.

"Right," Loshak said. "No evidence that robbery was a motivating factor."

A musty odor greeted them as they moved off of that square of linoleum and stepped into the house proper. Even though it had only been three days and nights since the murders took place, the air in the house smelled stale as though it had been closed up for much longer. It reminded her of the mildew stench of the bathrooms in her college dorm, freshman year. The janitors had tried their best to combat the issue, but it seemed that no amount of scrubbing and bleaching could clear that earthy yet acrid scent.

Cherry wood floors gleamed everywhere, reflecting the gray light that slanted in all of the windows. This flooring ran through the kitchen to their immediate left and a hallway to the right, presumably leading to the bedrooms. And the nursery.

At the end of the hall, a large decorative mirror hung on the wall. It had been shattered into a thousand pieces, cracks emanating from a clear point of impact in the center. She raised her arm, phone in hand, and took a picture of it. Darger was gazing at her fractured reflection when Loshak spoke up from the kitchen.

"Mrs. Cameron was found here," he said, pointing to a throw rug in front of the kitchen sink. "Stabbed numerous times, mostly in the chest. She died before bleeding out, probably from loss of organ function, or possibly from shock."

Looking closer, Darger could see the discoloration tinting the hue of the dark rug, if only a touch.

"Postmortem, her abdomen was cut open from the belly button to the sternum," Loshak said. "And many of her internal organs — liver, spleen, pancreas, lungs — were stabbed numerous times as well."

His words conjured memories of the gory images she'd flipped through on the plane, the slit opening the woman's belly with a bulge of large intestine left hanging out, weirdly brown and purple. She'd never seen anything like that before.

Loshak hesitated a moment, seemingly waiting for her to chime in. Darger didn't know what to say, though, so she said nothing. She only lifted her phone and snapped a few photos.

"So that's pretty, uh, unusual," Loshak said, finally.

He turned and moved a few paces into the dining area. Darger followed.

"Mr. Cameron was found here. Under the dining table," Loshak said. "He, too, was stabbed multiple times. Too numerous to count. Based on the spatter evidence, it's thought that — wounded and in shock — he crawled under the table, where he eventually died of blood loss."

The off-white carpet sported a rust colored splotch about the size of one of those bearskin rugs Darger remembered from the old Westerns she'd watched with her dad growing up. And she could see the trail of spatter leading off into the living room, arterial spray most likely, all of it brown with a ruddy hue. The sound of her camera's shutter punctuated the silence.

"I'm not judging any murder victim," Loshak said. "But I hope it was already over when he came here and hid. I hope he didn't leave them..."

They both stared at the brown spot on the floor for a long silent moment before Loshak led the way into the bathroom.

The room was dark for a moment as Loshak fumbled for the light switch, and the mildew smell was stronger here. It filled Darger's nostrils with a stink strong enough to make her eyes water a little.

The fluorescent bulbs flickered and came on, buzzing a little. The broken mirror over the sink distorted her reflection. It was an eerie image, her face splintered and cracked and stretched out of proportion. When she tore her eyes away and looked down, it was a second before she made sense of what she was seeing.

Gummy blood pooled on the linoleum floor. Thick. Opaque. A mottled skin had formed along the top of it, and its shade was much redder than the stain on the carpet. A deep, cloudy red, like wine going almost milky from sitting out for too long. This patch of blood alongside the bathtub wasn't nearly as big as that splotch under the dining table. It was, she supposed, about the height of a child.

"And this is where Ellie, the six-year-old…" Loshak said, trailing off and leaving that sentence unfinished. "Multiple stab wounds, again. Too numerous to count, again. These lacerations were focused not on the abdomen such as in both parents' cases, however, but on the face and eyes. Police recovered the tip of the murder weapon — a standard, mass-produced kitchen knife — in this room, where it broke against the victim's cheekbone."

She couldn't help but imagine the sound that might make. Metal breaking against bone.

This time they didn't linger in the vicinity of the blood mark. Darger shuffled out of the bathroom as soon as Loshak finished speaking, and he sniffled a little as he followed her, flicking the lights off as he passed through the door.

For the first time since they'd entered the house, Darger led the way. She moved down that cherry floored hallway, the white bedroom doors closed before her. The nursery would be last, she realized. The most gruesome of the murders would be their final bit of work here. Perhaps that was for the best.

They glanced into the other two rooms, the six-year-old's bedroom and the master. Both neat to an uptight degree apart from the child's unmade bed.

And now her hand gripped the cool metal handle of

the nursery door. She swallowed and felt a lump in her throat. Her wrist rotated, and she stepped forward, applying pressure on that thin rectangle of wood that separated her from the scene of the horror. The door stuck in the frame for a moment, jerking free with a loud pop that startled her.

Goose bumps pulled her skin taut all over, and she found herself staring at the floor. She could vaguely make out the white frame of the crib, the row of ornate wooden bars, almost like an altar centered along the back wall of the room, but she couldn't look at it directly. Not yet. She saw it only as a blurred shape at the top of her field of vision.

There was less light in this room, and for a moment Darger worried that Loshak would turn on the light as he had in the bathroom. He didn't.

They took careful steps into the nursery until they stood over the baby bed, and then they stopped, first him and then her. They didn't speak. They didn't move. The whole house went utterly still for a long moment. They stood in that silence, the atmosphere heavy with some blend of awkwardness and reverence. A suffocating sense of terrible, terrible loss.

"The infant..."

Loshak stopped there, his lips moving a little. Was he searching for the right word? Overcome with emotion? She couldn't say.

"They found a portion of the infant's remains here. In the crib. Most of the, uh, corpse was not recovered."

Again the talking cut off, and Darger let herself look.

There was surprisingly little blood in the crib. Just a single smear. A curved red line that stretched over the fleece blanket and onto the sheet.

And she thought about the details that Loshak was unable to say out loud: A flap of the baby's scalp had been recovered at the scene, along with enough skull fragments and brain matter for his death to be a foregone conclusion, even without the body to verify it.

She didn't want to, but Darger raised her phone and captured the image of the bloody crib, her hands and arms shaking all the while.

CHAPTER 4

Neither of them spoke much on the ride away from the house. Loshak put his window down, and the white noise of the air flowing in seemed to drown out any need for talk.

The wind flipped Darger's hair around, the cool of it cutting through to her scalp so the top of her head tingled like mad.

She sketched a profile in her head without really thinking about it, the internal monologue somehow distant, as if the voice in her head was not her own. She was thankful for that, though. For the roar of the air keeping the awful reality at arm's length.

The unknown subject would be a white male in his mid-twenties. His appearance would probably be noticeably disheveled. Unkempt. Poor hygiene. Probably on the excessively thin side. He'd almost definitely have a history of mental illness, and history or not, he'd exhibit erratic, paranoid behavior at the least, with delusional thoughts and actions being very, very likely on top of that. This would be a loner, someone with almost no relationships outside of his immediate family. He'd be unemployed, probably having been so for the majority of his adult life. He'd live alone within a couple miles of the scene of the crime, and police would almost surely find evidence of the crimes out in the open in his residence. His home, like his personal appearance, would be disorderly.

Messy. And a history of drug use was probable as well.

Was that it?

She tumbled the details around a moment.

Yeah. Yeah, she thought that was it.

She watched the wind move the pine boughs around, all the trees shaking their limbs in unison like a group of children on a playground.

She looked at Loshak, wondering what he thought of it all. He'd slid on a ball cap to keep the wind from wreaking havoc on his hair, and between that and the sunglasses, he looked like he was outright trying to hide at this point.

Once more they loaded the rental car onto the ferry, waiting in the line of cars for their turn to drive into the gloomy parking level in the bowels of the boat. The windows provided enough sunlight to see just fine, but it felt so much like being in a small parking garage instead of on a ship. Darger didn't think it was something she could ever get used to, not that she would get the chance.

With the Altima in place, Loshak killed the engine and peered at his watch.

"Ferry will be leaving in ten minutes, and we'll be there in forty. Anyway, I imagine we're on the same page," Loshak said, lowering the sunglasses at last. Tiredness showed itself in the lines puckering around his eyes, and she was reminded again that he'd only been out of the hospital for a little over a month.

She considered his question for a long moment before she answered.

"Yeah. I think we are."

CHAPTER 5

It was after noon when they reached San Juan Island, and Loshak steered them to a small diner with a view of the harbor. Darger hadn't thought she would have much of an appetite after the crime scene, but the smells coming from inside The Starving Barnacle changed her mind. They ordered and then sat at one of the picnic tables out front to eat. Well, Darger ate. Loshak mostly pecked at his salad and drank a lot of water.

"Still haven't got your appetite back?" she asked, thinking that maybe a roundabout approach was the way to ask about his health.

"That and the doctors got me on a real restrictive diet. Low fat and all that."

His nostrils flared as he gazed down at the pile of greens and vegetables on the plate.

"Apparently diabetes is a real risk for me now, so I gotta be careful."

"Ah," she said through bites of her fried fish sandwich. She almost felt a little guilty about eating something so comparatively decadent in front of him now.

"Honestly, I was a little surprised you were back at it so quickly. To work, I mean."

"I could say the same for you," he said, eyes flicking to her left arm.

She followed his gaze to where the bullet fired by

James Joseph Clegg had grazed her arm. She'd been lucky. The bullet had missed the major nerves and arteries. She'd have a scar, but it could have been much worse.

She shrugged and tried to keep a straight face. "Flesh wound."

Loshak snorted out a laugh.

"Anyway, it's not as if I had a choice."

Darger wiped her fingers on a paper napkin and arched an eyebrow at him.

"What do you mean?" she asked.

"You think I'm hot to go jettin' around the country so soon after all that? I was still officially on leave when they dropped this in my lap," he said, tapping the file he was balancing on his lap while he ate.

"Let me maybe correct your thinking on something, Darger. If you think the FBI gives a rat's hiney about your health, you can forget that right now. If you've got a pulse, they expect you to be going about business as usual."

Was that why she was here, she wondered? Babysitting again? But no, it was different this time. Loshak had been the one to invite her. And OK… maybe he had done so because he wasn't feeling one-hundred percent. That still meant something. It meant he trusted her. Right?

Loshak's voice interrupted her musing.

"You hear from the young Detective Luck since you left Ohio?"

She stopped chewing abruptly, realized what an obvious tell that was, and forced herself to continue macerating the French fry between her teeth. She dabbed at the corner of her mouth with her napkin.

"No. Why would I?"

She'd intended her voice to come out cool and impassive. But she couldn't help but think she'd sounded a touch defensive.

Loshak's eyebrows peeked up from behind the mirrored lenses of his aviators.

"Just thought maybe he might have been in touch. Case is closed, but that doesn't mean all of our questions were answered. I imagine they'll be sifting through the life of James Joseph Clegg for some time yet," he said. "It's not unusual to keep each other in the loop, you know."

Now she was curious. Casey had suggested they keep in touch. As friends, he'd said. Darger thought that was a bad idea, and said so. Needless to say, she didn't think she'd be hearing from him anytime soon, whether it related to the job or not.

"Well has he called you to give any updates on the case?"

Loshak took a swallow of water before answering.

"Nope."

He turned his attention back to his salad, and Darger watched him for a while, wondering why he'd brought it up at all. Professional curiosity about Clegg? Or was he hinting that he knew about her and Luck? Knowing Loshak, it was a bit of both. Meddling bastard.

She took a big, juicy bite of her sandwich, and this time she savored it without the least bit of guilt.

CHAPTER 6

The sheriff's office was too hot. Darger felt her cheeks flush within a minute or so of entering the room, and now she sat before the large desk, staring into the face of Sheriff Spencer Humphrey, finding it mustached, tan, and pudgy. His round face and the bleached highlights frosting his dark hair made her think of Guy Fieri.

"I won't lie to you," he said, his top lip freezing in an odd position that exposed his big Chiclet teeth for a moment. "We are out of our depths, but I look at it as a learning opportunity, yeah? We want you to handle the questioning of the subjects, if you would. And we'd like to observe the interrogations. If that's OK?"

Loshak's hands clasped in his lap, falling into slow motion wringing.

"That's not really..." he said. "I think maybe there was a miscommunication on the service the Behavioral Analysis Unit typically provides."

"Look, I know this isn't normally how you work," the mustached officer said. "But, just between us, we're in way over our heads on this whole deal. We could really use the help."

Loshak exhaled, long and slow. Darger couldn't tell if he was frustrated or bewildered. Perhaps both, she thought.

"I understand," Loshak said. "We can handle all of the questioning, and then we'll turn it over to the

Sheriff's Department from there."

The Sheriff sat forward in his seat, his meaty forearms leaning against the lip of his desk.

"Well, we've got six suspects we can tie to the scene, five of them the day of the crime, and they're all here, ready to talk to you."

Loshak flopped three of the folders on the desk.

"Anyone over thirty can go now," Loshak said, and then he looked at Darger. "Agreed?"

She nodded, and they both looked at the Sheriff. His mouth hung open as his eyes flicked from left to right and back.

"Well, now," the man said, adjusting in his seat. "That'd cut the number from six down to three. I mean… Are ya sure?"

Loshak's hand-wringing intensified. He licked his lips before he answered.

"Yes, sir. I'm sure. What we do isn't an exact science, but the probabilities are on our side. I can assure you of that."

The Sheriff ground his fingers into his mustache, staring off into space for a long moment, his eyes glassy.

"Just seems crazy is all. They came all the way down here and waited. Shouldn't we just talk to everyone? While they're here, I mean."

"I'm not telling you or anyone how to run the investigation, but you asked for our help. We're trying to give it to you. This is what we do. We use behavioral profiles to streamline the investigation. Let's trust the process, yes?"

As he spoke, Darger noticed the sound of Loshak's hand rubbing, a whispering noise like sheets of construction paper sliding against one another. If he was as frustrated as that sound suggested, he was good at keeping it out of his voice.

"I guess you're right," the Sheriff said. "I mean, of course you're right. You all are the experts. We'll do it your way."

☾

Darger and Loshak sat in a conference room, reading through the suspect files, which were pretty underwhelming. They had all given very basic statements, and the police had the suspects fill out additional forms about their backgrounds while they waited.

"I kind of figured we'd talk to the nephew first," Loshak said, and he turned to Darger. "What do you think?"

"He seems to fit the profile pretty well. History with drugs. He's on an antipsychotic medication, which obviously suggests some kind of psychiatric issue, though we don't have much to go on beyond that."

"Yeah, he's the only one we have any kind of psych history on, so I don't know. Figured we'd see what he said and go from there."

Darger nodded, and they got up to head for the interview room.

"How do you feel about all of this?" Darger said, almost under her breath. "The way they're handing the interrogation over to us and all? That's not normal, I'd imagine."

"It's unorthodox, but maybe it's for the best. I can't speak for the others, but the Sheriff here had no law enforcement experience before he took the job last year."

Darger's jaw dropped open.

"What? Are you serious?"

Loshak nodded.

"You see that from time to time in some of these smaller counties around the country. They're elected officials. No experience or qualifications required. Just votes. And this is a low-crime area. Mostly traffic enforcement, with a burglary here and there."

CHAPTER 7

The first subject, Jarold Cameron, sat in the interview room, forearms resting on the wooden table. The first thing Darger noticed was his hair. Shaggy red locks covered his forehead and encroached on his face. The fluorescent lights gleamed off of his pale skin, though the sides and back of his neck shone with raw patches of bright pink surrounded by peeling flakes of dead skin. Sunburn. A bad one, by the looks of it.

He was skinny. Not quite as emaciated as the unknown subject Darger had imagined in the car, but very, very thin. Sinewy. Stringy muscle tissue and veins shifted under his skin as he extended his hand to shake Loshak's and then hers. Weird how that worked, she thought. How some people's skin seemed to make what was going on underneath so plain to see. Maybe it was a lack of body fat more than a characteristic of the flesh itself. That would make more sense, and yet she couldn't quite believe it.

At 24, Cameron already had quite a history with drugs and alcohol. He'd racked up six counts of Minor in Possession of Alcohol before he made it to 21, and in the three years since that momentous birthday, he'd gotten popped for drunk driving twice. Three marijuana possession charges had been spread evenly among all of the alcohol charges, presumably to help keep things fresh.

She and Loshak sat across from Cameron, and

something about the chairs and table and fluorescent lighting reminded her of sitting at a lunch table in high school. Maybe the suspect himself was part of that — a scrawny ginger who wouldn't look out of place in the cafeteria even at 24 years old. She scooted her chair up to the table, metal legs scratching at the tile floor, and Loshak cleared his throat.

"I was sorry to hear about your aunt and uncle," Loshak said. "The kids, too, of course."

Jarold's eyes went wide, and he looked like a little kid himself, scared and alone among the adults. His lips twitched a few times before he settled on what to say.

"Yeah, it's too bad," he said, finally.

"So I hear you were over at their house that afternoon. Returning a…"

Loshak, of course, knew exactly what Cameron was there for. Darger figured he must be lulling him into participating in the narrative. She decided to let the senior agent press the action. She'd jump in when it felt right.

"Wave runner. I'd borrowed Uncle Ed's wave runner."

"Little cold out for that now, isn't it?"

Cameron chuckled a little, his face conveying more terror than humor.

"I'd had it since the summer. Ed figured with the new baby… I mean, they knew they weren't going out anytime soon is all. So he offered to let me borrow it a few months back. Let someone get some use out of it."

"Did you?"

"What?"

"Get any use out of it?"

Another terrified titter of laughter.

"Oh, right. Well, a little. I have a hard time with the sun, you know? I pretty much turn as red as a lobster if I spend more than 20 minutes out there."

"You gotta load up on the SPF 45, man."

"I do. Believe me. I slather it on like butter. Just doesn't seem to help. I don't know. I went out a few times, but…"

"Uh-huh. So you returned the wave runner. About what time was that?"

"It was after lunch. Around 2 PM, I guess."

"And was your uncle there?"

"Yeah. Yeah, they were all there. The whole family, I mean. I said hi to everybody. Ed came out and opened the garage so we could put the wave runner in there, and then I left."

"In a hurry?"

This time Cameron laughed longer, almost seemed to choke a little on the clucks emerging from his throat.

"No," he said, and Darger thought she could see tears in his eyes but just for a second.

Loshak stared at him for a long moment.

"Is something about all of this funny to you?"

The terror-laugh expression intensified on Cameron's face, but no chuckles came with it this time. Just a tiny gasp.

"No, sir. Just… I get nervous is all. Uncomfortable, you know? Feels like I'm getting called down to the principal's office or something, and I kind of feel like I'm going to get in trouble even though I didn't do anything. Other people don't get that? Me, I get all frazzled in this kind of situation, and sometimes the nerves make me laugh. Over-stimulation or something. Other times, I can't stop talking. I just jabber on and on about nothing. Like right now, I guess."

His ramble stopped abruptly, and the ensuing silence seemed strange. Awkward. Loshak and Darger both kept quiet, letting the tension build.

"So you didn't always get along with your uncle, did you?" Loshak said, his voice softer now.

A strange sequence of facial expressions contorted Cameron's features.

"What? Oh."

Again a pregnant pause reigned over the room. Cameron took a few deep breaths before he went on, the air hissing out of his nostrils changing pitch each time.

"You're talking about the fight?"

"That's right," Loshak said, without missing a beat.

"That was just family stuff, you know. It probably looked worse than it really was. Just family stuff."

"Look, I understand how it is. I've got family, too. So why don't you just talk me through it, for the record, so we're all on the same page?"

Darger looked at Loshak, almost expecting him to give her a wry look out of the corner of his eye, but he didn't.

"I loved Ed. Everyone did. But he had a temper, ya

know? One time I was with him out to the convenience store by the ferry landing. We were picking up a few things. Party supplies, I guess, for a little family reunion thing we do every 4th of July."

"And this would be the Cameron family reunion?"

"That's right. About twenty of us, I guess. Anyway, I grabbed the wrong paper plates. Ed wanted the segmented kind, you know? Like a school lunch tray or whatever. Styrofoam or whatever. But I just got the round paper kind."

"And that caused a fight?"

"Yeah. Well, I mean, I may have gotten mouthy with him, too. It wasn't just him that started it."

"Did it get physical?"

"No. Well, he shoved me a little, and I kind of went after him, lunged or whatever, but he kept me away long enough for me to think better of it. Nothing serious. Nobody landed a punch or anything."

"And this was right in the convenience store? Where people could see you?"

"Right. We were at the checkout counter. The clerk was there. A few other customers, maybe. I remember that my elbow knocked into a display of beef jerky or something. Slim Jims, I think. The real long ones. The little cardboard box holding them toppled over, and they spilled onto the counter. It was pretty embarrassing. For both of us, I mean. Ed got all quiet after that. I could tell he felt dumb about it."

"Did he apologize?"

"No. He didn't say much of anything for a long time. I don't think he was real big on apologies."

"Did you have any other encounters like that?"

Cameron took another deep breath, the wind inflating his chest and seeping out of him slowly.

"I mean… I guess so. We never got in a real fight, but he'd lose his temper, and I don't know. I guess it's not my nature to back down. But I mean, we were family, you know? It was never… I never even hit him. It wasn't…"

Darger saw this moment of vulnerability as her opportunity.

"On the form, you mentioned that you're on a prescription medication," Darger said, looking down at a sheet of paper to check the name. "Risperdal? How long have you been taking that?"

Cameron's eyes flicked toward the ceiling as he thought about it.

"A little under a year, I guess."

"That's an antipsychotic. Mind if I ask why it was prescribed to you?"

"I have OCD. Obsessive compulsive disorder, you know? The doctors have tried all kinds of treatments. So far this pill has worked the best."

Darger scrawled notes on the legal pad.

"I see. Thanks, Jarold."

Loshak leaned in, resting his forearms on the table.

"How did things seem at the house that day?"

"What do you mean?" the kid asked.

"You know, the vibe. They were your family. You know what they were like. Anything seem off?"

Cameron scratched his right nostril.

"Not really," he said. "Actually, I guess my uncle

was a little worked up, now that I think about it."

"Worked up, how?"

Cameron's finger stopped scratching abruptly.

"He was yelling."

Loshak looked up, intrigued.

"At you?"

"No. Someone came to the front door when I was there. Didn't see who it was. But I heard my uncle tellin' someone to get their ass off his property or he'd be callin' the cops. Called whoever it was a lowlife."

"What time was this?" Darger asked.

"I dunno. A few minutes after I got there. 2:05, 2:10?"

"And you didn't see anyone else when you left?"

Cameron shook his head, blinking rapidly.

"I'm not tryin' to be rude or anything, but will I get to go soon? I don't know anything that will help ya, or I'd tell it."

"I'll tell you what, just hang tight for a little longer," Loshak said, glancing at Darger, who nodded. "We might have a few more questions for you before we're done."

Everyone stood then, and Darger's legs felt stiff and strange. She had a sense of waking from a deep sleep, of vast amounts of time passing, though she knew it had only been a few minutes.

Cameron left the room first, escorted by one of the deputies. The FBI agents lagged behind.

Loshak stopped a few paces into the hallway, and after looking around to ensure he was out of earshot of anyone else, he spoke to Darger in a low, even voice.

"What did you think?"

"He fit the profile in some ways, but I'm not sure. The medication fits, but OCD wasn't exactly what I had in mind."

"Yeah," Loshak said, fingers pawing at his jaw. "Yeah, that's pretty much what I thought, too."

Loshak led the way through the doorway into the little observation area on the other side of the two-way mirror. The Sheriff sat at a small table there with a menagerie of deputies milling around, filling the small space almost entirely.

The body heat was oppressive, Darger thought, moist and disgusting. It was like walking into a sauna of mustached man-sweat.

The Sheriff's eyes lit up when he saw the FBI agents enter the room, a toothy grin stretching out beneath his mustache.

"Any thoughts, Agent Loshak?" Sheriff Humphrey said.

"Yeah," Loshak said, some sardonic trace in his voice. "I think I'd like to talk to the next subject."

The Sheriff's smile faded a notch.

"You know, one of the guys we sent away had a, uh, domestic violence conviction a couple years back. Beat up his girlfriend pretty good. He was a family friend who had visited with the Camerons the morning of. I can't help but wonder what he might say if you were to get him talking."

Humphrey trailed off there, and Loshak just stared at him, his face expressionless, his eyes dead. The silence in the room stretched out into something awkward, everyone holding still. Darger could see the muscles in her partner's jaw tense and release over and over again. Finally, the Sheriff spoke.

"But that's neither here nor there, I guess. We're happy to follow your lead and see this thing out, like I said."

"Yes," Loshak said. "Let's get on with it."

He turned his gaze from the Sheriff to look at the second subject, now sitting on the other side of the glass.

"What can you tell me about this guy, Walker? The lawn guy, is that right?"

"Yes, sir. And there's not much I can tell, I'm afraid. We've had a bit of trouble getting a hold of his parents, and he's… Well, he talks, but he doesn't say much, if you catch my meaning. I guess you'll see that for yourself."

CHAPTER 8

According to his file, Raymond Walker was 27, but he seemed like a kid in most every way Darger could see. The cut of his t-shirt seemed to make the sleeves ride up on his shoulders, revealing nearly the full length of his stick-like arms. His dirty blond bowl cut fell somewhere between Luke Skywalker and early Justin Bieber. And his lips hung open perpetually, revealing his bottom teeth, a chapped mess of white flakes hanging from the slack pink flesh like hangnails.

He certainly seemed to fit the profile physically, Darger thought. Disheveled. Underweight. Aloof. She looked into his face in that instant as they entered the interrogation room, though, and she couldn't get much of a read on him.

Walker didn't rise to shake hands as Jarold Cameron had. In fact, he barely reacted to Darger and Loshak's entrance apart from swiveling his eyes to glance at them for a moment before returning his gaze to the shiny tabletop in front of him. This was strange behavior, of course, but his energy was more meek than hostile, Darger thought.

The FBI agents sat across from the withdrawn man, and once more Darger had to remind herself to not think of him as a boy. He was only a few years younger than her, after all.

"How ya doin', Raymond?" Loshak said, sounding much more casual than he had in the earlier interview.

Walker didn't look up from the table as he answered, his voice coming out pinched and tiny.

"Good."

"That's what I like to hear. Do you know why you're here today?"

The slender man blinked a few times, his eyelids sticking a little each time they slid over his wet eyes. Something about it reminded Darger of wonky windshield wipers on a car. Walker didn't answer the question.

"Well, someone hurt your neighbors, the Camerons, and we're trying to figure out what happened. We just need to ask you a few questions, and you can go. I understand you were at the Cameron residence two days ago?"

More blinking, more thinking. Walker nodded.

"What were you doing there that day?"

"I cut the grass."

"And they pay you to do that for them, correct?"

He nodded.

"So you're over there, what, every week? Every other week?"

"Every Friday. After Dr. Phil."

The lightest puff of laughter exited Darger's nostrils, and then she fell into a sniffle to try to cover it up, fingers splaying around her nose to itch it.

Loshak smirked at her before he went back to asking questions.

"Who set that up? Did they ask you to mow their lawn? Did you offer them your services?"

"My dad told me to. He talked to them, I guess."

"I see. And how did you receive payment? From Mr. or Mrs. Cameron directly?"

Walker dabbed a finger under his eyelid as he answered, gaze still fixed on the tabletop.

"Mrs. Cameron gave me $20 whenever I finished mowing. I knocked on the door, and she gave it to me."

Darger scrawled a note, blue ink carving tiny grooves in the yellow legal pad before her: "Check TV listings for time of Dr. Phil." Something about writing the words "Dr. Phil" unleashed a strange giddy feeling in her belly, almost made her chuckle again, but she held it in.

"So Mrs. Cameron paid you on Friday afternoon?"

"Well, yeah."

"Did you see anything out of the ordinary, perchance?"

Walker thought about it, blinking away once more.

"No."

"Did Mrs. Cameron seem upset, maybe? Scared? Distracted?"

Walker swallowed, his throat clicking a little.

"No. I don't remember."

Loshak shifted in his seat, butt swiveling to reset the position of his legs.

"How long do you think it takes you to mow the Cameron lawn?"

"I don't know."

"Is it a big yard?"

"No. It's just normal."

Loshak nodded in slow motion.

"Have you ever been in trouble, Raymond?"

Walker's pause was his longest yet. When he spoke, his voice got even tinier.

"Yeah."

Loshak and Darger both inched forward in their chairs.

"What happened?" Loshak said, his voice falling into a hushed place to match Walker's.

"I threw away… I hid all of my broccoli in my napkin and threw it away. My stepmom. She saw me, and… But it wasn't like… It was because…"

Walker's demeanor seemed to shift before their eyes as he spoke, his forehead and nose wrinkling up like some snarling beast's.

"Raymond," Loshak said. "I was talking about legal trouble. Have you ever been-"

"Wait," Darger said, holding up a hand. "Why didn't you eat your broccoli?"

Walker looked up at her, their eyes connecting for the first time. His head twitched then like he was remembering something important, and all of the wrinkles in his face smoothed out.

"I just don't like broccoli. It's gross."

Darger looked at Loshak, whose brows crinkled into a puzzled look. She shrugged.

"You've never been in trouble with the police?"

He shook his head.

"So what'd you do after you finished mowing? Go home?"

"Yeah. I went home."

This was Walker's quickest answer yet, and he even

looked at Loshak, though he didn't maintain eye contact. Darger wasn't sure what to make of that.

"Did you stop and get paid first?"

"Well, yeah."

"Knocked on the door?"

"Yeah."

"Who answered?"

"Cindy."

"Mrs. Cameron?"

Walker nodded.

"Did you see anyone else? Mr. Cameron? The kids?"

Walker thought again, just for a tick. He shook his head back and forth.

"And everything seemed normal?"

He nodded.

"So you finished mowing the lawn, got paid. What did you do with the lawnmower? Do you bring your own or use the Camerons'?"

The blinking seemed to intensify.

"I use theirs."

"Did you put it away when you finished?"

"Yeah. In the garage."

"Was the door unlocked or did someone have to let you in to get the mower?"

"I have... Cindy gave me a key."

"To the garage?"

"Yeah."

Loshak nodded, letting up for a moment. A quiet settled over the room, and Walker seemed to grow uncomfortable. Fidgeting in his seat. His eyes locking onto the tabletop again.

Darger piped in.

"Raymond, can I ask if you have any history of mental health issues?"

He blinked again. Shook his head.

"No trips to psychiatrists or anything like that?"

He shook his head again, and Loshak and Darger locked eyes for a moment. Darger wasn't sure what to make of the weary look in the folds about Loshak's eyes. Was it related to the case? Or was he just wearing down after the flight and all of this extra police work they hadn't been anticipating? He really should be taking it easier. A little pang of anger shot through her when she thought of Loshak being ordered back to work.

She took a breath and fixed her attention back on their subject.

"Do you have many friends, Raymond?"

"Not really. I had friends before we moved, but…"

"So you grew up somewhere else?"

"Bellingham," he muttered.

"And you moved here with your parents?"

He closed his eyes as he nodded.

"Ten years ago," he said.

She waited, in case Loshak had more to add

"I think that's all for now," Loshak said. "Thanks for your time, Raymond."

☾

Once again, they found a quiet corner where they

could analyze what they'd learned.

"He fits the profile in some ways," Darger said. "Not in others."

"No history of mental illness."

She glanced down at the notes scribbled on the yellow paper.

"He could be undiagnosed. The social withdrawal and flat affect could be signs of something on the schizophrenia spectrum or maybe a mood disorder."

"Maybe," Loshak said, stroking his chin. "That's a big maybe."

Darger tapped her pen against her legal pad.

"I know."

They heard the sound of a door opening and the squeak of shoes on tile, and then the Sheriff rounded the corner.

"There you are," he said. "It was like I said, wasn't it?"

"What's that?" Loshak asked.

"The Walker kid. Kind of a closed book, am I right?"

"I suppose so."

Sheriff Humphrey's tongue snaked out of his mouth and slithered over the big white teeth.

"I was wondering if you had any insight you might like to share? So far, I mean."

He cleared his throat and continued.

"We're just all a bit anxious to find who did this, of course."

Loshak sighed.

"I understand that, Sheriff. But it doesn't behoove

the process to start floating theories before all of the evidence is gathered. Now if you don't mind, we're nearly done."

The Sheriff opened his mouth to speak but seemed to think better of it. Instead, he nodded once and headed back to the observation room.

Darger's eyes followed the man as he disappeared through the threshold. She wondered if Loshak's shortness was in part because he wasn't feeling well. He answered that when he popped two ibuprofen in his mouth and swallowed the pills without water.

Turning to her, he said, "Let's finish this, shall we?"

CHAPTER 9

Pete Malaby was more heavily muscled than both of the other subjects put together. He wasn't toned, Darger noted, his thick arms and neck somehow lacking any definition. He was just big and broad. The flesh itself was shapeless to the point that his wrists almost looked like a baby's.

He smiled when the agents entered the room. His skull was just as broad as the rest of him — the big round face swaddled with well-tanned flesh. It wasn't a chubby face. Not exactly. The skin just seemed plumped and darkened all over, like a hot dog that swells when you cook it.

They shook hands, his massive baby arm pumping Loshak's and then hers, the smile shifting a little on his face but never quite fading.

"How ya doin'?" he said, nodding at each of them.

"Doin' well," Loshak said, matching Malaby's enthusiasm.

"Same here," Darger said. "You?"

"Could be worse. I've been sitting down here at the cop shop for about three hours now, but, you know, it could be worse. Probably."

"Well, you should be out of here soon," Loshak said. "We appreciate your patience."

"No, I understand. It's terrible what happened. I don't mean to make light of it or anything."

He nodded to himself.

"Real shame, especially for it to happen to someone like that."

"Someone like what?" Darger asked, careful to keep her voice light. Mildly curious.

"Cindy. Mrs. Cameron, I mean."

She resisted an urge to glance over at Loshak. She knew he was thinking the same as her: why refer to the crimes as if there had been only one victim?

Loshak's voice was calm when he asked the next question.

"So you knew her well?"

Malaby brought a fist to his mouth and cleared his throat.

"No. Not really. I only meant to say, she was a nice lady. And good-looking, you know?" he said, then added, "For an older lady."

"And what about Mr. Cameron?"

"Not really my type," Pete Malaby said, adding a rakish wink. A laugh that sounded more like a grunt rumbled from the back of his throat.

"Cute," Loshak said.

"Sorry, I got kind of a sick sense of humor sometimes."

The thick muscles on either side of Malaby's neck bunched when he shrugged.

"Mr. Cameron seemed like an OK guy."

He coughed again.

"Can I get you something to drink?" Darger said. "Water? Coke? Maybe a coffee?"

When he spoke his voice sounded a little hoarse.

"No, thank you. I'm fine."

"An OK guy?" Loshak repeated. "That's it?"

"I mean, he was one of those Seattle types, right? You know how they are."

"Actually," Loshak said, "we don't. We're not from around here. Could you elaborate?"

"Just that they're uptight, you know? They want their steaks free-range and grass-fed and all that. I mean if you're gonna go to all the trouble, why not throw in a little Asian masseuse action, a little Happy Ending before the cow gets slaughtered, am I right?"

The grating laugh came again, and Darger gripped her pen so hard she thought it might snap in half. But she was supposed to be the good cop here. Or at least the quiet cop.

"There's that sense of humor again," Loshak said. This time he smiled a little.

"When you do your deliveries, do you bring the paper to the door? Or is there a delivery box you leave it in?" Darger asked.

"Some people got a box. But a lot of them just have me leave it on the porch."

"Do you knock when you drop it off? Let them know it's there?"

"No, ma'am," Malaby said. "I start my route at 5 AM, and a lotta people would be mighty pissed off if I was ringin' their doorbells at that hour."

Darger nodded.

Loshak spun a pencil between his fingers and then tucked it behind one ear.

"You ever had any problems there at the Cameron place?"

"Not really."

"No complaints about your service?" Loshak pressed.

Malaby lifted a hand to scratch at the back of his neck, eyes wandering to the ceiling as if deep in thought. His attempt to appear nonchalant was almost comical. He clicked his tongue.

"You know, there was one little thing. I mean, it's nothing really. But the husband did one time kinda get on my case."

"What about?"

Malaby cleared his throat.

"I barely even remember," he said, squinting like he was viewing the memory through a thick haze. "Oh right. So us delivery drivers can sign up for what's called a 'supplemental.' It's a sort of mini paper some of the local newspapers put out to try to attract new customers. It's mostly ads. Anyway, it's a way to get some extra scratch. Everybody gets that one, subscriber or not. But there's no box for it, so I just toss 'em next to the mailbox."

He rubbed his hands together.

"Mr. Cameron didn't like that. Called it littering," Malaby said and rolled his eyes. "Said it got all soggy when it rained, and he just ended up tossin' it anyway. Like I said, Seattle types."

"And when did this altercation take place?"

"Altercation? Nah, man. It wasn't like that."

Loshak raised his eyes to meet Malaby's.

"Disagreement, then?"

"Yeah, sure," Malaby said. "Couple weeks ago, I

guess."

Darger almost snorted but held back. With all his melodramatic reflection, she would have thought it must have happened a year ago.

"And that was that?" Loshak asked.

"Pretty much."

"Things went back to normal after that?"

"Yup."

"You went back to delivering the supplemental to the Cameron house the same way as before?"

"No," Malaby said. "If people ask us to stop, we're supposed to take them off the delivery."

"Were you aware that Mr. Cameron filed a complaint about you with your employer?"

"I might have been aware of that, yeah."

"Might have?"

"OK, yeah. I was. But it was bullsh- I mean, it wasn't true. I stopped delivering the supplementals there," he said, jabbing a finger on the table top. "You know what I think? I think he found a pile of old papers. I don't always have the best aim when I'm tossin' the papers out, so I think he found a stash of old ones he'd missed before. Then he calls my boss and tells him I'm still litterin' in his yard? That's bull."

"Then what?" Loshak asked.

Malaby shrugged again, and Loshak fixed him with a hard stare.

"You know he accused you of smearing his paper with dog shit?"

Malaby's lips pressed together in a hard line. "Yeah."

"Did you?"

"Hell no," Malaby said, rubbing at the back of his neck. "I wouldn't do somethin' like that."

"Were you angry about it?"

"About him reportin' me to my boss for stuff I didn't do? Of course I was."

Malaby's cheeks were colored with pink blotches now.

"Let's go back a little ways," Loshak said.

He opened the file in front of him and peered down at a piece of paper. It was out of Malaby's line of sight, but Darger recognized it as the fingerprint comparison sheet.

"You said you don't ring any doorbells when you do your deliveries."

"Right."

"Can you explain then, why we lifted one of your prints from the doorbell of the Cameron house?"

Malaby tried to keep cool, but Darger saw the first twinkle of panic in his eyes.

"I don't... how..."

"You have a record, Pete. Your DUI from a few years back. We've got your prints on file."

Another cough erupted from his throat, and he looked to Darger.

"Could I get that water now?"

Loshak rapped his knuckles against the tabletop to redirect his attention.

"In a minute, Pete. But right now, I think you ought to explain to us how it is that your fingerprints got on the Cameron house doorbell if you — as you've said yourself — don't ring the doorbell."

Malaby's jaw started working back and forth.

"Man, this is bullshit," he said finally.

"What is?"

"You think I killed them, is that it? Guy's a prick to me, calls my fuckin' boss tryin' to get me fired, and so I killed him and his whole family?" Malaby said, his voice getting steadily louder until he was almost shouting. "That's fucking crazy!"

"Then tell us what happened."

Loshak's voice was level.

Malaby's eyes were wide now.

"I just— I wanted to talk to the guy is all. Explain things," he said.

"And did you? Talk to him?" Loshak asked.

"Yeah. I said my piece, and then I left."

"So you didn't have an altercation? Didn't shout at Mr. Cameron?"

Malaby clenched his hands into fists and slammed them onto the table.

"Goddamn it! You keep doin' this! Asking me questions you already know the answer to!"

Loshak, voice still calm as could be, stared at him.

"Listen, Pete. The only thing we're interested in is the truth. So if you'd start tellin' it, we're all ears."

"Fuck you!" Malaby shouted, banging his meaty hand into the table again. "I'm done. I want a fuckin' lawyer!"

Darger exchanged another wordless glance with Loshak. In unison, they got up and left the interview room.

☾

Instead of heading straight to the observation room where the Sheriff was surely waiting on pins and needles, Darger and Loshak took a moment to compare notes. Little discussion was necessary, it turned out. They'd come to the same conclusion.

"I don't think we're looking for some cold-blooded killer so much as we're looking for someone who needed help and didn't get it," she said.

Loshak pinched the flesh between his eyes.

"Wouldn't be the first time, sadly," he said.

They were hovering over the files for the three men they'd interviewed when the conference room door swung open, and Sheriff Humphrey strode in.

"Well," he said, "that was enlightening."

Loshak turned to face him, arms crossed over his chest.

"Yeah?"

"I did the preliminary interview with Malaby myself. Seemed like a jovial kind of guy. Never would have guessed he was such a hothead."

Loshak said nothing. The Sheriff raised his eyebrows, looking hopeful.

"I assume you've decided, then?"

"We have," Loshak said.

He flipped the nearest folder shut and extended it to the Sheriff. When Humphrey read the name on the label, his mouth popped open. He closed it and glanced up at Loshak.

"You're sure about this?"

Loshak's head bobbed once.

"And we're fairly confident that if you search his residence, you'll find plenty of evidence."

The Sheriff swiped a hand over his mouth, still staring at the manila folder.

"I'll call in for the warrant right now, get things rolling," he said, starting for the door.

He paused with one hand on the door handle and turned back.

"You'll stay, though? If we do make the arrest, I'd be much obliged if you were here to get a confession. Or try to, I should say."

"Might as well see it through," Loshak said.

Darger couldn't help but think that Loshak didn't sound thrilled about the prospect.

CHAPTER 10

By the time Loshak and Darger headed back into the interview room, it was late. She supposed it was officially an interrogation room now. Two of the witnesses had been sent home hours ago. Just one remained, and he was now more than just a person of interest.

Raymond Walker sat in the interview chair once more, staring at his blurred reflection on the glossy tabletop. He looked more haggard than he had that afternoon, the wrinkled flesh beneath his eyes going purple.

Darger laid out pictures on the table before the boy. Pictures of Raymond's apartment, which police had just spent the last four hours searching.

Blood spotted the beige carpet in one. A crusted knife, tip broken off, sat on a battered coffee table in another. A t-shirt drenched in red rested in a wadded up ball on the floor. It went on and on. Images of the overwhelming physical evidence filled the table block by block.

She hesitated when she got to the last picture in the folder, recoiling at the sight of it.

The baby's body lay wedged at the bottom of a plastic garbage can, curled into the fetal position. It was so small and pale. A powerless little creature.

The police found the trash receptacle under the kitchen sink. Thrown away with the table scraps of

Walker's most recent meal — fish sticks and macaroni.

No one spoke when she was finished laying out the pictures. The quiet filled the space with incredible tension.

Raymond rocked back and forth a little in his seat. He still stared straight at the table, his face blank. Darger couldn't tell if he was processing the photographs before him or not.

Loshak cleared his throat and spoke.

"Why don't you tell us what really happened, Raymond?"

The rocking stopped, and the flesh on Raymond's forehead wrinkled. After a moment he shrugged and started shifting himself back and forth again, slower this time.

"You made no attempt to conceal your crimes. The bloody clothes. The knife. The body. We know some of what happened. We just need you to fill in the blanks so we can all go home."

Raymond's expression didn't change.

Darger decided to chime in, hoping to simplify the line of questioning.

"Did you do that to the Camerons, Raymond?"

The head bobbed on the scrawny neck.

"Can you answer aloud, yes or no?"

"Yes."

"You killed them?"

"Yes."

Loshak sat forward in his seat, nodding for Darger to keep going.

"Can you tell me why?" she said.

No answer. Just rocking back and forth.

"Did the Camerons do something to you?"

"Yes."

"What did they do?"

Silence.

"Did they hurt you?"

"Yes. Well… maybe."

"Did they try to hurt you?"

"Yes."

"How?"

"Poison. They were trying to poison me."

Loshak and Darger looked at each other.

"How was that?"

"The gas for the lawnmower. Poisoned. It was lowering my blood."

The room fell quiet again.

"Lowering your blood?" Loshak said.

"I needed their blood. Because of the poison. I needed more blood, or I'd die."

Darger thought a moment.

"Were other people trying to poison you as well?"

"Yes."

"Is that why you didn't want to eat your broccoli?"

"Yes."

"What about the mirrors?" Loshak said. "Why break them all?"

"Oh, they can watch everything through the mirrors."

Raymond lifted his head to tilt it toward the two-way mirror before he went on.

"Like the police watching through that mirror right

now? Just like that."

Darger watched the three of them in the glassy reflection.

"Can I get my mac and cheese now?"

Loshak and Darger looked at each other.

"What?" she said.

"I'm hungry," Raymond said, again looking at her for the first time.

"What's he talking about?" Loshak said.

She shrugged, glanced back into the mirror as though an answer might appear there, projected onto the silver rectangle.

There was a knock on the big metal door a moment later. Three soft thuds. And then the door inched open, Deputy Sumlin's sheepish face appearing there.

"It's about the comment he just made. He, uh, had a pocketful of macaroni and cheese. When we brought him in, I mean."

"We're talking about a wad of cooked noodles, right?" Loshak said. "Not a box or package."

"Right," Deputy Sumlin said, licking his lips. "It was a bunch of loose noodles, smeared in cheese sauce. Kraft, from the looks of it. A big handful of the stuff just jammed into his pocket or something. I don't know."

Loshak and Darger looked at each other again.

Raymond smiled.

"Gotta be careful what you eat these days. I made it myself, so I know where it came from."

☾

The next morning, the sheriff's department gained access to Walker's medical records, which documented his long history of mental health issues. After killing a few pets in the neighborhood, he'd been hospitalized at Western State Hospital in Lakewood for over a year. He turned 22 in the institution.

He was mostly a trouble-free patient, though he did manage to kill a couple of birds in the yard during rec time. Both times, orderlies found him in his room with dried blood caked all around his mouth, a bird corpse tucked under his mattress.

Eventually, though, the doctors had prescribed a cocktail of psychotropic medication that seemed to be working. He stopped trying to catch birds near the feeders, stopped talking about blood. They released him after two months without incident, saying he was no longer a threat to society.

And maybe that was even true for much of the past six years, but Raymond hadn't taken any of his pills in some time. He'd started to think they were lowering his blood.

☾

By the time deputies were poring over this information, Loshak and Darger were on the flight home.

For the first hour of the flight, Loshak napped. Darger sat bored and restless, alone with her thoughts. But now he was awake, sipping ginger ale out of a small plastic cup.

"Listen, I can get you transferred to the BAU," he said. "If you want it."

Her eyes opened a little wider.

"Even with Cal Ryskamp blocking the way? I've known him a long time. He's not exactly the forgiving type."

Loshak scoffed.

"The pissant bureaucrats like him always talk big, but believe it or not, there are people at the top who care about things like results. I happen to think you're good at those."

Darger looked out the window at a gray sky, puffy clouds sprawled out all around them. For a while, the only sound was the low hum of the plane's engines. She swiveled back toward him.

"Well, I do want it," she said. "I thought you didn't do the whole partner thing, though."

Loshak let out a long sigh.

"It's time for a change, I suppose. Need to make sure there's someone to pass the torch to and all that."

"Jesus, Loshak. You make it sound like you're dying."

He fixed her with those pale brown eyes.

"No. Not yet," he said and then took a swig of soda. "I guess technically I did die in Ohio, but... It didn't take."

Darger leaned forward a little in her seat, not quite able to restrain herself from asking a follow-up question.

"How was that?"

"Death? I don't know. I always thought it would be

this dramatic scene, you know? A clawing, ripping fight. But it actually turned out to be relatively easy."

The conversation died after that, and Loshak's chin slowly drifted back down onto his neck pillow.

When he was out, Darger eased past him and moved down the aisle toward the bathroom. She didn't know why. She just wanted to be alone.

The BAU. This was what she always wanted, but it felt different now that it really was happening. Staring death in the face with Victor Loshak — this was her life now.

Flashes of gummy blood on tile came to her all at once, and she shuddered a little as she locked the bathroom door, shoulders doing that fast motion shimmy. The odd feeling didn't change once she was sealed in the restroom like she thought it might.

She looked at herself in the mirror, listening to the endless low-pitched hum of the plane's engines. A warped spot in the glass rippled the flesh of her forehead, made one eye look bigger than the other.

It made her look like someone else.

THANK YOU

Thanks so much for reading *Image in a Cracked Mirror*! Want more Darger books? Leave a review on Amazon, and let us know.

A NOTE FROM THE AUTHORS

Unfortunately, Amazon won't automatically flag you down when there's a new book in the *Violet Darger* series. Don't miss out!

Here are two ways you can make sure you're always among the first to know what Darger and Loshak are up to:

1) Sign up for the Vargus/McBain email list and never miss a new release. Just visit: **http://ltvargus.com/mailing-list**

2) Follow one of us on Amazon. Just click the **FOLLOW** button under my picture on my author page, and Amazon will send you an email every time we have a new release.

ABOUT THE AUTHORS

Tim McBain writes because life is short, and he wants to make something awesome before he dies. Additionally, he likes to move it, move it.

You can connect with Tim via email at tim@timmcbain.com.

L.T. Vargus grew up in Hell, Michigan, which is a lot smaller, quieter, and less fiery than one might imagine. When not click-clacking away at the keyboard, she can be found sewing, fantasizing about food, and rotting her brain in front of the TV.

If you want to wax poetic about pizza or cats, you can contact L.T. (the L is for Lex) at ltvargus9@gmail.com or on Twitter @ltvargus.

LTVargus.com

Printed in Great Britain
by Amazon